BABES IN TOYLAND

Tom-Tom

Contrary Mary

Mister Barnaby

Jane

Alan

Delancey Marmaduke

The Widow Piper

Roderigo

BY JAMES HOWE

ILLUSTRATED BY ALLEN ATKINSON

Babes in Toyland

BASED ON THE OPERETTA BY

VICTOR HERBERT AND GLEN MACDONOUGH

GULLIVER BOOKS

HARCOURT BRACE JOVANOVICH

San Diego   Austin   Orlando

Gonzorgo

Grumio

The Master Toymaker

Requests for permission to make copies of any
part of the work should be mailed to:
Permissions, Harcourt Brace Jovanovich, Publishers,
Orlando, Florida 32887.

Library of Congress Cataloging-in-Publication Data
Howe, James.
Babes in Toyland.
"Gulliver books."
Summary: A retelling, based on the 1903 operetta,
of the classic story of how Jane and Alan are pursued
by their evil uncle Barnaby who wants to kill them
for their fortune.
[1. Fantasy. 2. Toys—Fiction. 3. Operas—
Stories, plots, etc.] I. Atkinson, Allen, ill.
II. Herbert, Victor, 1859–1924. Babes in Toyland.
III. Title.
PZ7.H83727Bab 1986 [Fic] 86-4640
ISBN 0-15-200411-4

Designed by Joy Chu
Printed in the United States of America
First edition
A B C D E

HBJ

STORYTELLER'S NOTE

From its Broadway opening at the Majestic Theatre on October 13, 1903, to its most recent re-creation as a Walt Disney film in 1961, *Babes in Toyland* has enchanted generations of children, young and old. Bringing together favorite characters from Mother Goose, young lovers in danger for their lives, villains, fairy spirits, dancing butterflies, and marching toy soldiers, this theatrical extravaganza caused one early critic to proclaim, "It will prove a perfect dream of delight to the children, and will recall the happy days of childhood to those who are facing the stern realities of life."

Quickly entering the mainstream of American culture, the Victor Herbert/ Glen MacDonough operetta was frequently revived on the stage in the early part of the century and provided the basis for several television productions in the 1950s, a popular 1936 MGM film starring Laurel and Hardy, and the 1961 film featuring Annette Funicello and Tommy Sands as the young lovers (the "babes" of the title) and Ray Bolger as the villainous Uncle Barnaby.

When I was asked to write the book version of the story, I was surprised to learn that none already existed, and even further surprised to realize that, familiar as I was with the title, I really didn't know what *Babes in Toyland* was *about*. The "March of the Toy Soldiers" came to mind, but beyond that, and a vague association with Christmas, I drew a blank. I was quick to learn that I was not alone in my shadowy awareness of *Babes in Toyland*, for what had once been one of the most popular pieces of family entertainment of the twentieth century had been virtually lost due to changes in theatrical style, popular taste, and financial wherewithal. Imagine a producer today capable of staging a four-hour spectacle with constantly changing costumes and sets and a company of 123—and all at a price affordable for the average family!

In re-creating *Babes in Toyland* as a book, it is my hope to bring this special story to new generations of children who, like me, enjoy fantasy, romance, suspense, and humor, and who may, as I did in writing it, hear the echoes of an earlier time when young lovers blushed and villains were hissed and a world of make-believe lay just beyond a red velvet curtain.

The curtain is going up. And the story begins again.

JAMES HOWE

CAST OF CHARACTERS

MISTER BARNABY, *a rich miser, in love with Contrary Mary.*

JANE, *his niece.*

ALAN, *his nephew.*

RODERIGO, *a sentimental ruffian.*

GONZORGO, *his hard-hearted partner.*

THE WIDOW PIPER, *a lonely widow with fourteen children.*

CONTRARY MARY, *her eldest daughter.*

TOM-TOM, *her eldest son.*

her other daughters	*her other sons*
BO PEEP	SIMPLE SIMON
JILL	JACK
MISS MUFFET	TOMMY TUCKER
SULKY SUE	PETER
CURLY LOCKS	BOY BLUE
POLLY FLINDERS	GEORGY PORGY

THE MOTH QUEEN, *a benevolent ruler fond of disguises.*

DELANCEY MARMADUKE, *a puppetmaster who is down on his luck.*

THE MASTER TOYMAKER.

GRUMIO, *his apprentice.*

THE ROYAL JUDGE OF TOYLAND.

MADAME GERTRUDE, *an opera singer.*

Party-goers, butterflies, citizens of Toyland, and Toys which possess the remarkable capacity to come to life!

snapdragons and nasturtiums, the goldenrod and periwinkle glow.

And what an exciting adventure had lain ahead. A sea voyage! Her dear uncle Barnaby, with whom she and Alan had lived since their parents' deaths, had arranged it all.

"An early Christmas gift," he had told them, pinching their cheeks just a little too hard in his enthusiasm.

When Jane had heard the knock on her door, she had known it was Uncle Barnaby, come to fetch her. She had hurriedly tied a ribbon in her hair, the peach-colored one trimmed in the very lace that had once formed the hem of her mother's wedding dress, and rushed to the door.

"How lovely you look," Uncle Barnaby had said, picking at his teeth with a used toothpick (he was a frugal man). "But hurry, child. The ship's crew is ready to depart. Your brother has already gone to join them."

The crew of the *Ladybug* consisted of two sailors. Roderigo and Gonzorgo were their names. They seemed kind enough, offering their two passengers a breakfast of kippers, hard rolls, and jam. Despite the ship's groans of age and protest, the voyage had been most pleasant until the clouds had gathered in the distance and the gentle breeze had changed to a stiff and chilling wind.

"Better go below, you two," Roderigo had called out. "Looks like a storm's brewing."

They had quickly done as Roderigo told them, seeking shelter from the darkening skies in the cozy cabin below. It was not until much later, when the storm raged and the ship was being tossed about like a child's toy, that they had come up to look for the sailors. And found that they were gone.

Forced to take refuge on the open deck, they had waited for the winds to die down. When Jane felt her brother's hand loosening about her shoulders, she opened her eyes.

"Let's go below and look for the others," said Alan. "Undoubtedly they came to help us and were forced to stay below when the storm got so bad. Keep hold of my arm. And whatever you do, don't let go."

In the cabin, the two called out the sailors' names.

PROLOGUE

ALAN AND JANE ARE DISCOVERED AT SEA,
AMIDST THUNDER AND LIGHTNING.

THE OCEAN FOAM spewed upon the decks of the *Ladybug* as Alan held tight to the mizzenmast of that once venerable ship. He was not sure how much longer he could last against the merciless storm, but he knew that for the sake of his dear sister, Jane, whom now he clutched tightly against his chest, he must try.

The ship pitched forward and back in the ever-mounting waves, as the timber of her hull cracked and whinnied. Jane did not speak or even try; she thought only of the cold and lonely death surely awaiting her at the bottom of the sea. Even if she had wanted to speak, her voice would not have been heard above the howling winds and pounding rains, the terrifying explosions of thunder that sounded as if the world itself were coming apart.

She closed her eyes and forced herself to think back to the promise with which the day had begun. She remembered standing at the little window, the only window, in her room, watching the children at play in the garden below. How bright the morning sun had been; it had made the

BABES IN TOYLAND

from his lips, "when you come looking for us, you will find your lost sheep."

"That isn't funny," said Bo Peep. The other children tried hard not to laugh. "Mary wouldn't let you say such things to me if she were here. Oh, Tom-Tom, where *is* Mary?"

Tom-Tom tightened the scarf around his sister's head. "You know Contrary Mary," he said. "Mother told her to stay at the party. So, naturally, she went for a walk."

"She's so lucky to be older," Curly Locks remarked. "She can do whatever she wants. And one day soon, she'll marry and never have to listen to Mother again."

"I wish we were big like Tom-Tom and Mary," said Tommy Tucker wistfully.

"Me, too," Polly Flinders said, wondering if her mother would notice the dirt she'd already managed to get on her freshly starched pinafore.

"You will *all* be big one day," Tom-Tom promised. "But for now, being little will make it all the easier to hide from Bo Peep. Are you ready, children? All right, Bo, you must count to ten and then come looking for us."

ONE

FROM THE VALLEY below Barnaby's house, from the very garden Jane had gazed upon earlier that day, laughter rang out like noonday bells. For here where the sun still shone and no one had the least inkling that there'd been a storm at sea, a party was in progress.

Tom-Tom, the oldest of the Widow Piper's fourteen children, was placing a scarf about the eyes of Bo Peep, the youngest. As the game of blindman's buff began, the other children teased their sister.

"We'll hide up on the hill," said Jack, with a nod to his twin sister, Jill. "You won't find us there."

"And you won't find me," said Simple Simon, "though I promise to play *fair*."

Sulky Sue began to cry, for she didn't know where she would hide. When Georgy Porgy tried to kiss her cheek, she pushed him away and cried all the harder.

"Perhaps, Bo Peep," said Peter, wiping the last traces of pumpkin pie

"Roderigo!"

"Gonzorgo!"

But their calls were met only with the creaking of the ship's timbers and the terrible sounds of the storm gathering strength once again above them.

"They're gone!" Alan said.

"And all our hopes with them, I'm afraid," said Jane.

"The poor fellows. They must have drowned." Alan took off his cap, out of respect for the recently departed, and wrung it out. "It's too late for them, Jane. We must now do whatever we can to save ourselves."

The ship lurched suddenly, and, with a great crack, water rushed into the cabin. "Look!" Jane cried. In the outer wall of the ship's hull were several large holes.

"Why, it's almost as if they'd been made there," said Alan.

"They have," Jane said. "The storm made them. Oh, Alan, what are we to do?"

"We must find a lifeboat. Hurry!"

But when they reached the upper deck, they found that the only lifeboat was gone as well. "It must have washed away," said Jane.

The ship rolled to one side. Alan and Jane skidded along the deck, nearly falling through the broken railings and into the ocean's depths. It was only a second roll in the opposite direction that saved them, allowing them to grab hold of the mizzenmast again. Their bodies shook with cold and fear. Jane began to cry.

"There, there," said Alan. "Everything will be all right. You'll see." But when a bolt of lightning splintered the very mast they were holding and tumbled its sails into the icy waves, he knew that there was nothing left to them but their prayers.

As Bo Peep began her counting and her brothers and sisters scattered about the garden, the rest of the partygoers, who until this time had been noisily chattering, suddenly grew still. The organ-grinder stopped his music. The ice cubes in the lemonade stopped their clattering. The only sound was Bo Peep's hesitant counting: "Five . . . six . . . six . . . what comes after six? . . . oh, I remember, seven . . ."

She did not see, as the others did, the entrance into the garden of the Widow Piper on the arm of Alan and Jane's uncle, Barnaby. Both wore their customary black: the widow out of mourning, the old man out of habit. But today they wore something else that the citizens of their little village were not as accustomed to seeing. Smiles cloaked their faces like veils.

"Nine . . . ten!"

Bo Peep, arms outstretched, began to roam the garden. Stumbling down a cobblestone path, she drew closer and closer to her mother, until . . . "I've found you!" she cried. But tearing the scarf from her eyes, her joyous cry turned to a surprised gasp. "Mister Barnaby!"

The Widow Piper's children gathered protectively behind Bo Peep. There was something about the old man that had always frightened them, and now there was something about the smiles on his face and their mother's that frightened them even more.

"Children," said the widow, "I hope your ears are clean, for Mister Barnaby has something important to tell you."

"Is it to do with Mother Hubbard?" cried someone in the crowd.

"We hear you evicted her from her home this morning," cried another. "And sent her poor dog to the pound!" An angry rumbling ran through the crowd.

"My good people," said Barnaby, who, because he was so very rich, managed to have a finger in just about every pie in town, "am I to blame if Mother Hubbard has not paid her rent? I am just upholding the law."

"And who makes the law?" shouted the organ-grinder. "*You* do!"

The rumbling of the crowd grew louder. Barnaby turned to the Widow Piper and shrugged. "You can't please everyone," he said.

"Yet everyone seems to be enjoying the party you've thrown," said the widow.

"This is *your* party?" asked Tom-Tom, quite surprised, for he had never known the miserly old man to give a party before.

"And what is wrong with that?" said Barnaby, stamping his foot.

"Nothing," Tom-Tom muttered to his brother Simon, "but if we'd known, we'd never have come."

"Mister Barnaby is giving this party," said the Widow Piper, "to celebrate his upcoming marriage."

"Oh, Mother," Bo Peep cried, running to the widow and grabbing hold of her skirts. "You're not going to marry Mister Barnaby, are you?"

The Widow Piper laughed. "Of course not, Bo. I married for money the first time. Now with your father dead, I shall marry for love. No, Mister Barnaby is to marry your sister, Contrary Mary."

It was the children's turn to laugh. "Marry Mary?" said Tom-Tom. "There's not a chance of it, Mother. What makes you think she will marry for money any more than you would?"

Emphatically, the Widow Piper replied, "Because I tell her to!"

"All the more reason she won't," said Tom-Tom. Then, slapping the befuddled Barnaby on the back, he said, "Cheer up, Mister Barnaby, we may be relatives yet. Even if you don't marry my sister, I hope one day soon to marry your niece, Jane. Think of it. You shall be my uncle, too. Will that be good enough for you, Mother?"

The veil-like smile returned to Barnaby's lips. "We shall see if you marry Jane," he said.

"Where *are* Alan and Jane, Tom-Tom?" said Bo Peep, tugging at her brother's shirt sleeve. "Why are they not at the party?"

"That's a question for their uncle," Tom-Tom replied. "Only he keeps such careful track of their whereabouts."

Before Barnaby could say a word, there came a sound so dreadful, a caterwauling so full of woe, that everyone turned to listen. It was a sort of sobbing, but a sobbing of such force that it barely seemed human. Yet human it was, for within minutes there appeared in the garden two sailors, one of whom was wiping his nose with a dirty red-checkered handkerchief.

"For heaven's sake," said the other, "you'll rust your waterworks if you go on like this, Roderigo."

"I can't help it," sobbed the one called Roderigo. He held something out and said, "Look at it, Gonzorgo, just look!"

"A bird's nest," Gonzorgo said. "What of it?"

"It tumbled out of the tree, and now the poor little bird doesn't have a home." And here the sobbing renewed itself with even greater vigor.

"Have you ever seen such a tenderhearted chap?" said the Widow Piper.

"That I am," Roderigo said, rushing to the widow's side.

"Why, I am so tenderhearted, it hurts me to kill time."

"Say," said Barnaby, looking Roderigo in the eye, "aren't you the same fellows I hired to take my nephew and niece on a sea voyage this morning?"

The two sailors nodded.

"Well, where are they?" Barnaby inquired.

Roderigo tried to respond, but his words were choked by his sobs, and tears ran down his cheeks.

"Raining again?" said Gonzorgo.

"Have you no heart?" Roderigo bellowed. "Oh, Mister Barnaby, we have such . . . such . . . *news*. How will you bear it? How can *I* bear to tell it? It's about the *Ladybug*. She . . . she . . ."

"What's happened?" Tom-Tom said. "Is Jane all right?"

"Let *me* tell," said Gonzorgo, "for my heart is locked in ice within this frozen bosom. Nothing touches Gonzorgo, lest it be a pair of saucy eyes . . ." And here he winked at the Widow Piper. "Or the touch of gold and silver on my palm." And he shifted his gaze, which turned hard as steel, to Barnaby.

"Perhaps we'd best discuss this privately," said the old man. And, bowing to the Widow Piper, he took the two sailors aside. The party-goers buzzed among themselves, while Bo Peep turned to her brother and asked, "Have Alan and Jane been lost at sea, Tom-Tom?"

"Worse, I am afraid," said Barnaby, turning back to the crowd. "My dear, dear nephew and niece have . . . how can I say it? . . . they've . . ."

"Drowned," said Gonzorgo. "And that's the truth of it."

"Drowned!" several voices cried at once.

"Oh!" cried Barnaby. "To think that they've been taken in the springtime of their lives. Nevermore to brighten their poor old uncle's dark and lonely days." The Widow Piper rushed to Barnaby's side, but he brushed aside her rather clumsy attempt to comfort him. "No," he said, "I must be alone. It is too much to bear my pain publicly. But my friends, don't let this little news spoil the party. Eat up! Enjoy!"

And off he went up the mountainside to his house, while Roderigo and Gonzorgo trailed behind, Roderigo sobbing all the while.

"Even I am not so simple as to think we can enjoy the party knowing that Alan and Jane are dead," said Simple Simon.

"Yes," Jill said. "It's not Mister Barnaby's loss alone. We all loved Alan and Jane. Alan was so handy. Who will repair our buckets now, Jack?"

"If you didn't fall every time we went up the hill, Jill," said Jack.

"*I* fall? You're the one—"

"Children, children," Tom-Tom said, "now isn't the time to argue." He drew the children to him so that no one else, not his mother nor any of the others at the party, could hear him say, "Besides, I don't know that we should believe Mister Barnaby."

"You don't?" said Miss Muffet.

"We shouldn't?" said Boy Blue.

"There is something suspicious about his grief," Tom-Tom replied. "You see, Alan and Jane once told me that they inherited a great deal of money from their parents. But it will not be theirs until they both have wed. Should they never marry, or should they die, their entire fortune will be Mister Barnaby's. You know what a greedy man he is." The children all nodded their heads. "What if he has taken them somewhere and is only telling us they are dead? What if he is trying to prevent my marriage to Jane?"

"And Mary's to Alan," said Jill. "For it's Alan she loves, even if she pretends not to."

"I must look for them," Tom-Tom said.

"But where will you go?" asked Simple Simon.

"I don't know. All I know is that I must find out the truth."

Just then, the Widow Piper called to her children to come in for their naps. Several of the younger ones followed her into the house, though Bo Peep was not among them, for she wanted very much to be like her oldest sister, Mary, and therefore tried to disobey her mother as regularly as possible.

"I'll leave at once," Tom-Tom said, "before Mother knows I've gone. Wish me luck, children."

"Good-bye, Tom-Tom!" the children called out as they watched their brother run off through the garden. "Good luck!"

Just as he was about to disappear from sight, Miss Muffet called out, "Don't go into the forest, Tom-Tom! It's full of spiders!" She shuddered at the thought.

But Bo Peep remembered something even worse. "Once you're lost in the Spiders' Forest," she said, "they say you can never find your way out. Tom-Tom, be careful!"

But they could not be sure that Tom-Tom had heard, for he was now lost from sight. And their mother was again calling from the house that it was time for all good children to come inside and rest their weary heads.

. —— .

TWO

THE SAILORS' NEWS fell on the party like rain. The crowd began to disperse, and the children, wondering when they would next see their brother Tom-Tom and fearing they might never see Alan and Jane again, turned with heavy hearts to go inside. But when they heard the sound of jangling tambourines and singing that was almost like laughter, they turned back.

"Gypsies!" Bo Peep cried.

And the party-goers, stopping in their tracks, echoed the word, "Gypsies!"

Moments later, two brightly costumed figures stood framed in the trellis entranceway to the garden. The children ran through the crowd to greet them. One of the gypsies was a boy who wore a red silk scarf about his head; the other, a girl, was draped in flowered and polka-dotted garments that might have been quite attractive had they not been worn together. As it was they were such a jumble of color and design, they made the eyes long for a darkened room. Both wore masks.

"Who are you?" Bo Peep said, gazing up at the exotic characters.

"And where have you been?" asked Tommy Tucker.

"We have been," said the boy, "at sea."

"At sea?" shouted someone in the crowd. "Did you witness the wreck of that good ship, the *Ladybug*?"

The gypsies lowered their heads. "We did," said the boy, in a mournful voice. "She was swallowed up like the moon on a cloudy night. One minute, she was there; the next, there was only the dark."

Bo Peep wiped away a tear. "Can you tell us what has happened to Alan and Jane?"

The girl knelt down by Bo Peep's side. "Don't cry, little one," she said in a soothing voice. "Alan and Jane are—"

"In heaven," said Simple Simon.

The boy laughed. "Heaven *almost* increased its population today," he said. "But fortunately those two had their wits about them."

"Not to mention their life jackets," said the girl. "In fact, Alan and Jane are nearer than you think." She removed her mask. The crowd gasped.

"Jane!" shouted Bo Peep, throwing her arms around the girl's neck.

"If this is Jane," said Simple Simon, furrowing his brow, "then it stands to reason that you must be—"

"Alan!" said the boy. He too took off his mask, and the crowd let out a great cheer.

"But why are you wearing masks?" asked Miss Muffet.

"And why these strange clothes?" Georgy Porgy said.

"Our life jackets kept us afloat for the longest time," said Jane, lifting up Bo Peep. "But when we were finally washed ashore, our clothes were all in tatters. We walked and walked and came at last upon a gypsy camp. There, the good people gave us fresh clothes and, as gifts, these masks and tambourines."

"After we left the gypsy camp, we couldn't keep from singing," Alan said, "for we're so grateful to be alive. And we put on the masks just now, thinking we might surprise our uncle Barnaby."

"He'll be so happy to see us," said Jane. "Where is he?"

Before anyone could answer, the Widow Piper's voice cut through the crowd like a wet knife through butter. "Children!" she shouted. "I told you to come in for your naps." Then, spotting Alan and Jane, but being a little nearsighted and taking in only their disguises, she cried out, "Ah, gypsies! Come, which of you tells fortunes? I want to have my fortune told."

"Watch me have some fun with your mother," Alan whispered to the children. He and Jane put their masks back on as he stepped forward and took the widow's hand. "*I* tell fortunes," he said, seeming to study her open palm. "Ah. Oh, dear. Aha!"

"What? What?" said the Widow Piper. "What is it you see?"

"You are a widow," said Alan. "You were married to a carpenter, but an oak log fell on him."

"Alas," the Widow Piper said, "it's true that the good Mister Piper is no more. He came to a hard wood finish. What else do you see? What of the future?"

"You have a daughter named Mary."

"Who is quite, quite contrary," said the widow, pursing her lips.

"Still, she is lovely," said Alan. "And she will marry a young man who is charming, gifted, and attractive. He is all that a young man should be and slightly more. To an outstanding character, he adds an unusual capacity for business and a brilliant future. His name starts with an *A*."

The Widow Piper pulled her hand away. "Perhaps you need glasses, my gypsy friend," she said. "For your vision into the future is blurred. I know of whom you speak—a nice enough fellow named Alan. But he was drowned at sea today. Besides, my daughter is engaged to marry another."

"Another?" Alan cried. "What do you mean?"

"Just that. She's to marry Mr. Barnaby."

"Uncle—I mean, Mister Barnaby!" Alan said. "It can't be!"

"It is, and what's it to you, gypsy?"

"Everything. That is, nothing. It's just that . . . it's just that—"

"It's just that he's never been wrong before," said Jane, coming to her brother's rescue. "Will you excuse us, kind lady? I think we'll be on our way." Under her breath, she said to Alan, "We must find Uncle Barnaby at once." And bowing to the crowd, they hastily departed.

"Hmph!" the Widow Piper muttered. "Gypsies! All right, children, you've had enough excitement. Into the house for your naps. And where, I should like to know, is Tom-Tom?"

"Tom-Tom!" the children shouted as one.

"We have to stop him," said Bo Peep excitedly.

"We'll go," said Tommy Tucker, grabbing Simple Simon's hand. And before their mother could even call out their names, they were gone.

THREE

BUT TOMMY TUCKER and Simple Simon did not find their brother that day. He was too far ahead of them, and besides, they were only allowed to go a few hundred yards from home and that took them just to the garden wall. With a boost from Tommy, Simon scaled the wall and scanned the horizon.

"Nothing," he said at last. Jumping down, he took his brother's hand, and together the boys walked sadly home.

By "nothing," of course, Simon meant "no sign of Tom-Tom." But he *had* seen three figures climbing slowly up a mountain road. He did not think much about these three, other than to assume that the one in black was Mister Barnaby and the other two the sailors Roderigo and Gonzorgo. He did not give any thought at all to what they might be saying to one another; and, even if he had, he was much too innocent a child to imagine just what a wicked turn their conversation had taken.

"You escaped," Barnaby said. "Are you sure the children didn't?"

"Quite sure," said Gonzorgo. "The hull of the ship was full of holes— *my* work."

Roderigo, who had just managed to compose himself after his histrionic display in the garden, said, "We waited till the storm was almost upon us, Mister Barnaby. Then we rowed away and turning back . . . turning back . . ." Here, he began once again to weep. "We saw the ship go down. It was such a touching sight I can barely stand to recall it."

"Then maybe you should sit," said Gonzorgo, shaking his head in disgust.

"So," Barnaby said gleefully, "I have seen the last of my little charges."

"Yes," said Gonzorgo. "And now you'll see the first of ours." And he handed him a bill.

Barnaby put on a look of surprise, as if the pleasure of having drowned two children should have been reward enough, but he said nothing, for just then he heard someone coming along the road. Seeing who it was, he said to the others, "Away with you, lads. Here's someone I must talk to."

"But—"

"Away, I say. We'll discuss the matter of your bill another time. Come to my house tonight—*after* you've had your supper."

No sooner had Roderigo and Gonzorgo left Barnaby's side than there appeared before him a girl wearing a red stocking on one leg and a yellow one on the other. In her hair were ribbons as mismatched as her stockings, and over her skirt she wore a petticoat. Only Contrary Mary could have made such an outfit fetching.

"Ah, Mary," Barnaby cried, reaching out his hand toward her, "a rose among the lilies, a pansy among the violets, a magnolia among the wisteria!"

"My," said Mary, "aren't you free with your flowers of speech."

"Eh?"

"But of course you are. They don't cost anything."

"Why, Mary, don't be hard on me," said Barnaby. "If only you'd seen the party I gave today. The extravagance of it! There were flowers . . ."

"It *was* in a garden," Mary said.

"And music."

"If the organ-grinder hadn't played, you'd have increased the cost of his license."

"But the refreshments!" Barnaby cried.

"Sour lemonade," said Mary. "I tasted it before I left."

"Just you wait," Barnaby said as he fumbled for Mary's hand. "When we are wed—"

Mary pulled her hand away and laughed. "Not that old song," she said. "I've told you before, Mister Barnaby, you may be the richest man in the land, but you are also the oldest. And the meanest."

"You could learn to love me."

"I was never very good in school."

"But, Mary, some day—far off—wouldn't you like to have your name on my family tombstone?"

"Please, sir, your efforts to improve your lot are in vain. I have given my heart to another—though he doesn't yet know it."

Barnaby began to chuckle. Then, wiping the grin from his face, he looked at Mary in mock sorrow. "If it is Alan you mean," said he, "I am afraid you'll find your plans are all wet."

"What are you saying?" asked Mary.

"Oh, my dear, sweet girl. My nephew and his sister drowned today."

"Drowned!"

Barnaby dropped his head and pulled a handkerchief from his pocket. "In water," he said, wiping his eyes. "I'm afraid you have no choice but to marry me now. Your mother has given us her blessing. In fact, she *insists* that we wed."

"All the more reason I shall never!" Mary cried. "Oh, my poor Alan. My dear boy! I will never marry you, Mister Barnaby. I don't know what I shall do without Alan. But I will never be so desperate as to sell myself into bondage for a band of gold."

Barnaby grabbed her and pulled her to him. "You're mine," he said,

his sentimentality replaced by a fierce determination. "You're mine, and there's nothing you can do about it."

Mary stepped hard on Barnaby's foot. He let out the sharp cry of a wounded puppy, and Mary bolted from him. He tried pursuing her, but a young girl (even one in mismatched stockings) is much too quick for an old man with a sore foot.

Contrary Mary was not sure where she was going. All she knew was that she would never go home again if home meant a life without Alan and an unhappy marriage to another. She ran like the wind, and didn't look back.

Had she turned back, she would have seen two masked gypsies approaching Barnaby on the road. She would have observed them remove their masks. And the surprise on the old man's face would have been matched only by her own. But, as it was, she missed Barnaby's reunion with his nephew and niece. And she carried the anguish of Alan's death with her as she continued on her unhappy way.

"We're alive, Uncle Barnaby!" Jane was saying. "Aren't you glad to see us?"

"G-G-Glad," Barnaby stuttered. "Glad is not the word."

"Poor Uncle," said Alan, seeing that Barnaby's legs were starting to shake. "You've had quite a shock."

"That," said Barnaby, "is an understatement."

"It must have been dreadful to imagine you'd have to spend the rest of your life alone," Jane said. "No wonder you proposed to Contrary Mary. It was an act of lonely desperation, wasn't it, Uncle?"

"Well, yes . . . I mean, no . . . that is . . ."

"Don't worry, Uncle Barnaby," said Alan. "You'll never be lonely again. And now you'll have no need to marry Mary."

"Oh," said Barnaby, unable to think of anything else to say. How, he wondered, would he be rid of these pesky children now? But when Alan spoke again, an idea presented itself.

"Come," the boy said, taking his uncle's arm, "let's go home. I can't wait to change into my regular clothes."

"Nor I," said Jane.

Barnaby stopped the children in their tracks. "We can't go home," he said.

"What's that?"

"What do you mean?"

"I mean," said Barnaby, speaking slowly in order to give his thoughts time to form themselves into words, "that we have no home to go to. Shortly after you left this morning, a terrible fire broke out."

"Oh, no!" cried Jane.

"How terrible," Alan said.

"Not quite as terrible as all that," said Barnaby. "I did manage to save everything of value. Nothing of yours, of course. But the house itself is gone. All that remains is a shell."

"What will we do now?" Jane asked.

"Oh, you know how resourceful I am, dear children. I have already bought a new home. In fact, your rooms are being painted now. I'm sure they'll be dry by tonight. Why don't you run off to the Widow Piper's and see if there aren't some clothes you might borrow? Roderigo and Gonzorgo will come for you this evening."

"Roderigo?" said Jane.

"Gonzorgo?" Alan cried. "Have those two good sailors survived? Oh, Uncle, how brave they were—they must have gone off in search of help when the storm was at its worst."

"They are courageous chaps, indeed. It was only a miracle that saved them."

"Just as a miracle saved us," Jane said.

"Yes," said Barnaby, scowling. "One miracle would seem all one could hope for in a morning." Then, changing his scowl to a smile, he patted Alan and Jane lightly on their heads and said, "Run along now, you two. And don't say a word about the fire. You know I can't abide being the object of anyone's sympathy. When the clock strikes seven, expect to see two sailors at the Widow Piper's door. They will see you safely to your new home. I'll follow in the morning."

"Then good-bye, Uncle," said Alan. "We'll see you tomorrow morning."

Watching his nephew and niece descend the mountain road, Barnaby laughed to himself. "You'll never see me, my lad," he said. "And you'll never see the morning."

FOUR

WHEREIN ALAN AND JANE ARE ENTANGLED
IN THE SPIDERS' FOREST.

THE SPIDERS' FOREST was cold and damp, and the tree branches so thickly woven above their heads that Alan and Jane could barely see the moon. Were it not for Gonzorgo's torch, the flickering fireflies would have been the only light upon their way. As she followed behind the sailors, Jane kept firm hold of her brother's arm, for she did not want to touch the slippery, moss-covered trees on either side of her or the sticky spiderwebs, which were so plentiful they made her wonder if anyone had ever been this way before.

"What a dismal place," Jane said to Alan, wishing she could ignore the hoots and cries that came at her from the dark. "And how easily we might become lost here. Do you think that's why Roderigo and Gonzorgo are leaving behind a trail of crumbs?"

"I suppose they want to be able to find their way back once they've left us at Uncle Barnaby's new house," Alan said. "I hope we get there soon. I'm so tired I'm ready to drop."

"It has not," said Jane, "been an ordinary day."

Ahead, Roderigo and Gonzorgo were engaged in a heated debate on the best method of carrying out their appointed task. The fingers of Gonzorgo's free hand nervously tapped the hilt of his dagger as he argued in a vehement whisper for striking quickly and having done with it. Roderigo favored leaving the babes in the clearing he'd spotted up ahead.

"After all," he said, his eyes brimming with tears, "there's no hope of escape from this foul place. If we weren't leaving a trail of crumbs, we'd never find our way out, either. Leave them, I say, and let them play as best they can whatever hand fate deals them."

Gonzorgo mumbled something his partner couldn't hear. "I tell you what we'll do," he said then. "We'll flip a coin. Heads, we leave them here. Tails, we slip some steel between their ribs, as Mister Barnaby instructed us to do."

"Agreed," said Roderigo, feeling in his pocket for the two-headed coin he always carried with him. Gonzorgo, onto his partner's tricks, unearthed a coin first. "We'll wait until we get to that clearing," he said, "where there's more light."

By the time Alan and Jane reached the clearing, they found the two sailors on their hands and knees, scouring the forest floor.

"What are you looking for?" Alan asked.

"A coin," Gonzorgo growled. "Roderigo dropped it."

"Is that it?" said Jane, spotting something glinting in the light of the moon. "How wonderful it is to be able to see again. I thought we'd be entombed in the darkness of this place forever."

"So you shall, so you shall," Gonzorgo muttered, picking up the coin.

"Eh?" Roderigo said.

"Heads," said Gonzorgo. "You've won." Then, to the children, he said, "Why don't you two take a little snooze? Roderigo and I don't mind stopping, do we, Roderigo?"

"I'd like to rest," said Alan, "if you're sure you don't mind." Roderigo and Gonzorgo smiled in response, and it was their smiles, turned sinister somehow in the shadows of the night, that Alan and Jane remembered as they drifted off to sleep.

So deep was their slumber that they did not hear the sailors steal away, kicking at the trail of crumbs as they went. When they awoke some time later, they were alone and hungry, and, though they wanted to tell themselves otherwise, they were beginning to feel afraid.

"I wonder where Roderigo and Gonzorgo have gone," said Jane.

"Undoubtedly to find us some food," Alan said. "They are such stout fellows. I'm sure they won't be gone long."

But as the night grew colder, it soon became apparent that Roderigo and Gonzorgo were not going to return.

"The poor s-souls," Jane said, her teeth chattering. "They must have lost their way."

Alan, who had placed his jacket about his sister's shoulders earlier, rubbed his hands together to keep warm. "I'm afraid if we try to go on without them," he said, "we too shall be lost. But if we stay here, we're sure to freeze to death."

Just then, some leaves rustled nearby. "They've come back!" Jane cried. But when she heard a growl most unsailorlike, and saw a pair of eyes squinting at her from the dark, she knew it was not Roderigo or Gonzorgo come with food but a beast looking for its dinner. She squeezed her brother's hand.

"If we remain still," Alan advised, "perhaps it will pass us by." In a moment (which seemed an eternity), Alan and Jane watched the animal's eyes narrow and widen. They heard its breathing and saw, or thought they saw, the vapor rising from its nostrils. A branch broke. The beast was moving. It was coming toward them.

Jane gasped. "Oh, Alan," she whispered. "We can't just sit here. We must try to save ourselves."

Alan nodded his agreement. "Keep hold of my hand. We'll stand up very slowly. Over there," he said with a nod of his head, "is a tree we can climb."

But as they edged their way across the clearing, their footsteps were echoed by rustling leaves and cracking twigs, their frightened gasps by angry growls. To their dismay, they saw that the pair of eyes that had stared out at them moments before was now multiplied tenfold. They were surrounded by hunger.

Reaching the tree at last, Alan's hand grabbed hold of a branch that came alive with a hiss and a wiggle and slithered away into the night. Swallowing hard, he tried to climb the tree, but his efforts were thwarted by the slimy moss that coated the trunk like a jelly. Jane, who no longer knew whether she shivered from cold or from fear, suddenly noticed the opening of a cave.

"Quick!" she said, pointing. "Let's hide in there."

But as they tried to enter (and as the forest around them came to midnight life with screeches and howls and hungry growls growing even hungrier), they were stopped by a large and sticky spiderweb stretching clear across the mouth of the cave. Alan raised his hand to strike the web, but Jane stopped him.

"There's a white moth," she said, "as badly tangled up in that web as we are in these woods. Oh, do set it free, Alan. I can't bear to see it struggle."

Alan knew that a moment's delay might cost them their lives, but the sight of the struggling moth stirred his heart. With gentle hands and a soothing voice, he began the delicate operation. "There, there, little creature," he said, even as the forest seemed to be closing in around them, "don't thrash about so. I'm not going to hurt you." Suddenly, the moth came free. High above their heads it flew, and, just when they thought it was going to disappear from sight, it came to rest on a log nearby.

And then the most peculiar thing happened. At least, it was a peculiar thing to Alan and Jane, neither of whom had ever been in an enchanted forest before and had no idea they were in such a place now. The air grew still. No leaves rustled and no twigs snapped and no unseen beasts growled. The eyes that had been peering out of the darkness at them were gone. The moth slowly closed its wings, and when it opened them again, a creature, tall and pale and beautiful, rose up and stood beside them. Except for the large white wings that grew from her back, she looked quite human.

"I am the Moth Queen," she announced. "You have saved my life, good children, and now I will protect yours."

Alan and Jane were so astounded they could not speak.

"In the guise of a tiny white moth, I was on my way to the world we call Outside when my old enemy, the Spider, trapped me in his web. Thanks to you, I am free."

The Moth Queen waved her arms, and the web disintegrated before Alan's and Jane's bedazzled eyes. Then she clapped her hands and cried out, "Butterflies! Come forth!"

Within seconds, the air was filled with butterflies, large and small, and of so many colors they seemed to make the night air shine and shimmer. "Take these children out of the forest," the Moth Queen commanded the butterflies. "To Toyland, take them!"

Turning to Alan and Jane, she said, "With these guardians, you will be protected from evil. But they will take you only to the forest's edge. Once there, you must protect yourselves." Then she smiled sweetly and took their hands in hers. "No matter what danger you find in this world," she said, "no matter what evil or what sadness, never harden your hearts. For it is a kind heart that offers the greatest protection of all. And now be on your way!"

And so Alan and Jane, amidst a flurry of dancing butterflies, bid the Moth Queen farewell and found themselves on their way to a place they'd long heard about but never imagined they would one day see with their own eyes—a place called Toyland!

FIVE

AFTER THE NIGHTMARE of being lost in the dark and dreary Spiders'
Forest, the brightly colored houses snuggled at the bottom of the hill were
a welcome sight. The distant clickety-clack of horses' hooves on cobblestone
streets, the clatter of milk bottles and wagon wheels, the flickering and fading
of street lamps all heralded the dawning of a new day. Curtains fluttered
lazily in half-open windows, as if the houses themselves were reluctant to
be roused from their slumber. And so the town slept, if only for another
moment or two.

It was in those moments, between no-longer night and almost morning,
that Alan and Jane ran down the hill from the forest's edge and slipped into
Toyland unnoticed.

Here was a place full of wonders—building-block bridges, oddly tilting
rooftops upon which whirligigs spun dizzily in the wind, and everywhere,
everywhere it seemed, Christmas trees hung with gingerbread men and
popcorn chains, shiny yellow stars and straw angels. Wandering its streets,

Alan and Jane felt exuberant and alive, for Toyland radiated the energy of a child on Christmas morning.

"Oh, Alan, isn't it wonderful?" Jane said. "If only Uncle Barnaby had let us come here—even once. But he always said the world was a dangerous place and we mustn't wander far from home."

"Perhaps he was right," said Alan, thinking of their recent adventures. "Still, I can't imagine any harm would come to us here."

Jane nodded. "Toyland is what a child might imagine heaven to be." Suddenly, she stopped and put her hand to her mouth. "Oh, dear," she said, "you don't suppose . . ."

"Suppose what?"

"You don't suppose we *have* died and gone to heaven, do you?"

Alan laughed. "Dying is not an experience we're likely to have forgotten," he said, putting his arm about his sister's shoulder.

Jane laughed, too. "I'm tired," she said. "Or perhaps Toyland is so like a dream, I'm no longer sure I'm awake."

Just then, they came upon a post that was covered with notices.

"Marmaduke's Amazing Puppets," one read. "They'll Make You Laugh, They'll Make You Cry. And All for One Stupendously Low Price. One O'Clock Every Afternoon in the Park—Now Until Christmas."

Another read, "Leash We Can Do, Incorporated—Dog Walkers. You Rest Your Feet, We'll Do the Rest."

But it was another that really caught their eye. "Only Four More Days to Place Your Christmas Order with the Toymaker! Don't Disappoint the Kiddies—Buy Them Even More Than Last Year!"

"I have an idea," said Alan, reading this last one aloud. "Let's get our Christmas gifts for the Widow Piper's children while we're here. What a surprise that will be—toys from Toyland!"

"It's a wonderful idea," Jane said. "I see only two problems."

"Oh?"

"First, we don't have any money. And second, we don't know the way home. We may never see the Widow Piper or her children again."

"Oh." Alan thought a moment, then said, "We mustn't lose hope, Jane. In such a place as Toyland, something good is bound to happen. Why, our fortune may lie around the next corner."

What *did* lie around the next corner was soon revealed to Alan and Jane, for just as they were about to turn it, they heard a familiar voice. "Now, children," the voice was saying, "I want you to look in every nook and cranny of this place, for I am sure this is where your brother and sister have come." The Widow Piper! Alan and Jane listened intently. "I don't know what possessed them to run away," the Widow Piper continued, "but I'll tan both their hides when I find them, you may be sure of that. They may think they're too old to be taught a lesson or two, but I will show them who knows best. I'll see to it that Mary is wed to Mister Barnaby yet."

"You said you were going to tan their hides, Ma," said Simple Simon. "Isn't one punishment enough?"

"We must find Mary and Tom-Tom before their mother does," Jane whispered.

"Let's hurry," Alan said, taking Jane's arm, "before we're seen."

The streets of Toyland were crowded with Christmas shoppers. In the squares and on the greens, acrobats and clowns entertained those who stopped to rest. A tiny train puffed and tooted along sidewalk tracks to carry others who did not want to take the time to rest but whose feet were tired from walking. Alan and Jane, exhausted after an hour of searching and having found no sign of their friends, wanted to climb aboard. But they had no money. And they no longer knew where to look.

"Let's go into this café," Jane suggested. "Perhaps the owner will give us some breakfast in exchange for our washing dishes."

"I *want* to keep looking," Alan said, "but if I don't eat something soon . . ." And here he stopped himself, for looking through the café window, he could not believe his eyes. There, eating biscuits and drinking hot chocolate, were . . .

"Mary!" Alan called out.

"Tom-Tom!" said Jane. And they rushed inside.

"Alan! You're alive!" Mary cried, so shocked she dropped her biscuit on the floor. The café owner's dog ran over and quickly disposed of it.

"I knew you were," said Tom-Tom, rushing to embrace Jane. "I never gave up hope."

"Are you glad to see me?" Alan asked Mary.

Mary returned to sipping her hot chocolate, slowly. "I am," she said, not wanting to give Alan too much satisfaction, "though I never doubted you were alive. But are you glad to see *me*?"

"Oh, yes," said Alan, his eyes lingering on the steam rising from Mary's hot chocolate.

"You look hungry, old man," said Tom-Tom. "Sit down and have something to eat. We have a little money left, enough at least to buy our friends breakfast. But we mustn't stay here long. There's danger in this place for you."

"And for you," said Jane, ordering a plate of eggs and biscuits and trying to ignore the dog's pleading eyes.

"You say there's danger?" Tom-Tom said.

"Yes, your mother, the Widow Piper . . ."

Thus did Tom-Tom and Mary learn that their mother and brothers and sisters had come to Toyland to take them home so that Mary might be forced into marriage with Mister Barnaby.

Tom-Tom said that they had nothing to fear from their twelve siblings; it was only their mother for whom they had to be on the lookout. But Alan and Jane had a much bigger worry, he told them. For he and Mary had seen Mister Barnaby with Roderigo and Gonzorgo here in Toyland. They didn't know why they were here, but they did learn that Barnaby had hired the two sailors to do away with his nephew and niece.

" 'Do away with?' " Jane asked. "Surely, you don't mean—"

"Murder," said Tom-Tom. Alan and Jane looked at him in shocked disbelief. "He wants your inheritance. I knew it all along. You must be careful not to be seen. He thinks—and they have given him no reason to believe otherwise—that Roderigo and Gonzorgo murdered you in the Spiders' Forest."

"Murdered us?" Alan cried. "Why, those good fellows would do no such thing. They left us to nap and went looking for—" Seeing Tom-Tom's incredulous gaze, he stopped himself. "They didn't go looking for food, did they? They left us to die."

Jane felt a chill run down her neck. "I can't believe it," she said.

"Nor I," said Alan. And then a new thought occurred to him. "The shipwreck," he said softly.

Jane looked at him with a puzzled expression.

"Don't you see? That shipwreck was no accident. It was planned. They put those holes in the side of the *Ladybug* and then took the lifeboat to save themselves. Oh, what a terrible thing when you can no longer believe in the goodness of your fellow man. Roderigo and Gonzorgo are nothing but paid assassins, Jane. And it is our uncle Barnaby who pays their bill. To think he wants us . . ."

"Dead," Jane whispered. That single syllable hovered in the air as a falling leaf hangs on the wind. For a time, no one spoke, and then Jane said, "I thought Toyland was a sweet place. Now I see that it isn't safe for any of us. It may be even more dangerous than the Spiders' Forest, for there at least we had the Moth Queen to protect us."

"And here we have each other," said Mary, taking Jane's hand.

Jane smiled. "I'm so glad we found you," she said. She shook her head as if to rid herself of her fears. "But how did you both get here? How did your mother? And Uncle Barnaby? Did you all go through the Spiders' Forest?"

"There's another way," said Tom-Tom. "It takes a day of traveling, but if you follow the river and cross the falls, you can enter Toyland through the Main Gate. They watch very carefully there to see who comes in and who goes out. You were lucky to have entered as freely as you did."

"Toyland is not at all the place you thought it to be, Jane," Mary said. "And not just because of Mister Barnaby's presence or our mother's. There is something . . . not right . . . here, though I cannot say what it is. Despite the Christmas trees and the festive air, there is an undercurrent of—"

Mary's words were interrupted by a sudden loud barking.

"What is it?" the café owner shouted. "What do you see, Rags?"

Through the window, there suddenly loomed a dark and ominous figure.

"It's Uncle Barnaby! And Roderigo and Gonzorgo are with him!" Jane said. "If he finds us alive . . . oh, Alan!"

Tom-Tom hastily paid the bill, and the foursome retreated through the back door, which the café owner was good enough to show them.

Outside in the street, Tom-Tom looked at the single coin in the palm of his hand. "I'm almost out of money," he said.

"And I," said Jane, "am almost out of hope."

"Yet there is one thing none of us is out of," said Alan. The others turned to him. "Danger," he said.

S I X

MOVING CAUTIOUSLY AWAY from the café, the four friends fell silent. Given the predicament they were in, it is doubtful that their thoughts were happy ones. Certainly they could not have been imagining the unlikely solution to their problems that fate held in store. For who, upon meeting the bent and gloomy figure of Delancey Marmaduke, would have envisioned him as a savior? Yet that is just what he proved to be.

They spotted him on a bench outside a big striped tent in the park. Even sitting down, he was a tall drink of water, as the Widow Piper would have said. The patches on his clothes indicated that he had known better times; the fact that the knees and elbows had been mended repeatedly showed that those times were long past. Holding his melancholy face in his hands, he stared at the ground and did not move except for an occasional sigh. Seeing him made Jane forget all about her own worries.

"What an unfortunate man," she said to the others. "If only there were something we could do for him." Then, spotting a sign near the tent, an idea occurred to her. "Look, here is where the puppet show is to be performed. And it's to go on in fifteen minutes. That would cheer him up. I'm sure he hasn't a penny. Tom-Tom, I know it's your last coin, but could you spare it for the sake of another's happiness?"

Tom-Tom didn't even have to think about his answer. "If it will make you happy, Jane," he said, "I'll do it." And marching over to the downcast soul on the bench, he held out his open hand and offered up its contents.

"Keep your currency, young man," the man on the bench said, with a long, drawn-out sigh. "There will be no performance today."

"How do you know?" Jane asked as she and the others came closer.

"Because I am the owner of those puppets. I," and here he stood to his full height of almost six-and-one-half feet, "am Delancey Marmaduke." He looked wistfully at them. "My tent is up and my tickets are sold, but my puppets have been seized by the officers."

Mary looked concerned. "What law have you broken?" she asked.

"There is a person here called the Master Toymaker," answered Marmaduke. "You may have heard of him. No plaything that does not come from his workshop may be shown in this country. Result, Delancey Marmaduke loses everything. Now I will have to return all the money I've been paid for tickets, and without my puppets I have no hope of making any more. And I did so want to buy myself a new suit of clothes for Christmas."

"Perhaps," said Tom-Tom, "someone else will give such a gift to you."

Marmaduke smiled sadly. "I have no one to give me gifts," he said.

"I wish we could help you," said Jane.

Alan thought a moment. "Perhaps we can," he said. "How many puppets do you need?"

"I could give a performance with as few as four," said Marmaduke.

"If I supplied them, would you make it worthwhile?"

"To you, a third of the receipts."

"Then here," said Alan, indicating himself, his sister, and their two friends, "are your four puppets."

"Oh, Alan!" Jane cried. "What a splendid idea!"

"I don't know," the puppetmaster said, scratching his head. "My story calls for three boys and a girl."

"I'm your man," said Mary, "for it's my very nature to be contrary. Nothing would make me happier than to be other than what I'm meant to be. But, Mister Marmaduke, we'd better hurry, for we've only ten minutes until the show is to begin."

"It just may work," said Marmaduke. "The play is short and won't take long to learn. Hurry inside the tent now and get ready. I have some costumes and, with some makeup, yes, yes, it just may work."

From backstage, the foursome could hear the audience arriving. "This is so exciting," said Jane. "And, Alan, you were so clever to think of it. Not only will we make some money now, but we'll be in disguise. No one will recognize us. Not the Widow Piper, not Roderigo or Gonzorgo, and, thank heavens, not even Uncle Barnaby." She put down her cake of rouge powder for a moment and wiped away the tear that had formed in her eye. "How sad it makes me to think that Uncle would want to kill us for the fortune Mother and Father left us. He has so much money now, what could he possibly want with ours?"

"There is something missing from his life," said Alan, "even with all his money."

"Perhaps," Mary said, "you should get him a kitten. How do I look?"

"Wonderful," said Jane. "You are the perfect soldier."

"And I?" Alan asked.

"The perfect soldier's mate. But, Tom-Tom, I do wish you didn't have to play the villain in the piece."

"It will be hard," said Tom-Tom, "to be evil to a heroine like you."

Just then, Marmaduke rushed in. He was pale and wiping beads of sweat from his brow.

"What is it?" Jane cried. "Are there so many empty seats?"

"Oh, no. They're gathering like ants at a picnic," he said. "In fact, I haven't a ticket left to sell."

"Are you worried about us then?" Alan asked. "Don't be. We'll be quite believable as puppets, even if we have no strings."

"I'm sure you'll be fine," said the puppetmaster. "It's . . . it's just that there's someone in the audience I didn't expect."

"Who?" Mary and Jane cried at once, Mary thinking it was her mother, Jane sure it was Uncle Barnaby.

"The Master Toymaker," said Delancey Marmaduke.

The four "puppets" looked one to the other. What if he tried to seize them, as he had Marmaduke's other creations?

Marmaduke said, "He asked me how it was I came to be performing this afternoon since he had taken my puppets this morning. I told him that I'd quickly made four new ones. He was so impressed that he said he must stay and see the work of such a gifted puppet maker. If he likes what he sees, he will let me keep my puppets and continue performing. If he doesn't . . . oh dear, I'm sure I don't know *what* he'll do."

Jane came forward and took the puppetmaster's hand. "Don't you worry,

Mister Marmaduke," she said. "We will make the Toymaker laugh."

"And we'll make him cry," said Mary.

"And," Tom-Tom said, "all for one stupendously low price."

Everyone laughed. And moments later the curtain rose on a play-with-puppets devised by Delancey Marmaduke for the entertainment of the citizens of Toyland, and presented here for the reader's amusement as well.

THE LASS AND THE BRASS

Featuring M A R Y as the First Soldier, A L A N as the Second Soldier, T O M - T O M as Captain Montmorrisey, and J A N E as Imogene Cassidy.

FIRST SOLDIER

Ah, 'tis a sad day for Imogene Cassidy,
Now that her true love has gone off to the war.

SECOND SOLDIER

She sits and she pines
And keeps lookin' for signs
Of Barney O'Flynn come knockin' at her door.

FIRST SOLDIER

But who is it knockin'? 'Tis not O'Flynn.

SECOND SOLDIER

'Tis Captain Montmorrisey, and she'd better let him in.

IMOGENE

Back, Captain Montmorrisey, your advances are in vain.

MONTMORRISEY

Don't defy me, lass, for my heart is split in twain.

IMOGENE

But I do defy you.
My Barney I would fly to.
You see, good Captain, my heart is already ta'en.

MONTMORRISEY

Another word and I'll call my soldiers to shoot!
They do what I tell them and are good fellows to boot!

IMOGENE

They look like good fellows to boot.

MONTMORRISEY

Since you will not have me, you've given me no choice!
Army, shoot the lady!

IMOGENE

Stop, and hear my voice!

FIRST SOLDIER

Do you wish to pray? Kindly don't take long.

IMOGENE

No, but I'm an Irish heroine, and cannot die without a song.

(sings)
Me heart have ye stole,
Yure the thief of me soul,
Me senses ye have taken, too.
Both fair Troyan Helen
And Venus excellin',
They'd ne'er hold a candle to you.

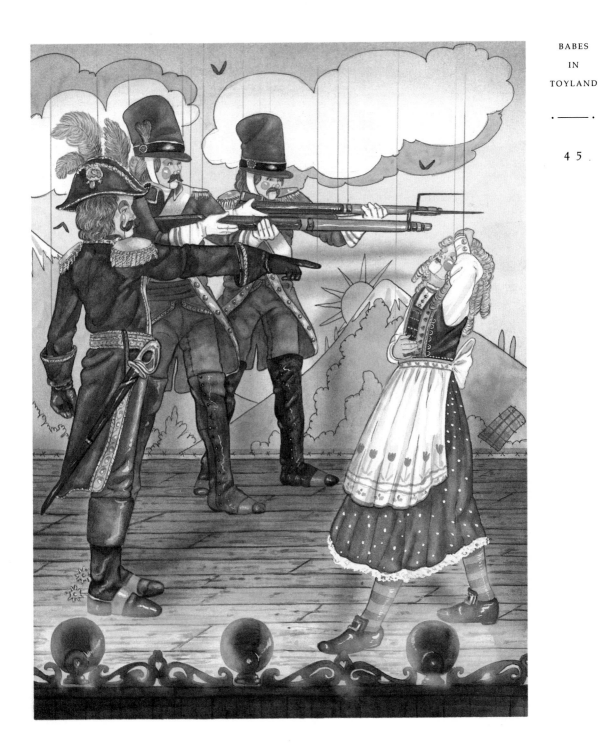

Oh, sweet Barney O'Flynn—

MONTMORRISEY

Enough! Shoot!

FIRST SOLDIER
(*tearfully*)
The Army cannot shoot a voice like yours, sweet lassie.

SECOND SOLDIER
And so we aim our rifles at he who's grown too brassy.

(*The Two Soldiers shoot Captain Montmorrisey.
They join Imogene in another chorus of
"Barney O'Flynn," and the puppets take
their bows.*)

— CURTAIN —

Backstage, even as the audience continued to cheer, the four "puppets" hugged one another jubilantly. Their performance had been a tremendous success!

Deliriously happy, Delancey Marmaduke rushed in and shook each of their hands in turn. "You've saved me," he cried.

"*You* have saved *us*," said Jane, "though you may not know it."

Marmaduke bowed modestly before continuing. "Not only was this the greatest show ever presented by Marmaduke's Amazing Puppets, but you have so impressed the Master Toymaker, he has requested a private performance in his home."

"When?" asked Mary.

"This very afternoon."

"How much?" Alan said.

Marmaduke smiled. "I asked for twice my usual fee," he replied. "And got it! Of course, a third of that is yours. Here." And, without ado, he dropped a heavy, jangling pouch into Alan's hands. "That is a third of the ticket receipts·and a third of the money just given me by the Master Toymaker."

"May we buy you a sundae?" Alan asked, suddenly feeling quite rich.

"It would be very pleasant to have someone buy me a sundae," said Marmaduke. "And when we've finished, I'll load you onto my cart—oh, excuse me, you were so convincing I still think of you as puppets. What I mean to say is, we will go at once to the Toymaker's home and workshop."

In no time at all, Mary and Tom-Tom, Alan and Jane, together with Delancey Marmaduke, proud puppetmaster, were pondering the vast selection of ice cream delicacies at the Toyland Sweet Shoppe. While in another part of Toyland, the Master Toymaker was pondering an altogether different matter.

SEVEN

''THOSE PUPPETS,'' said the Toymaker to his aging apprentice, "are the most remarkable I've ever seen."

Grumio, whose eyes were fixed in a permanent squint from years of dim light, nodded solemnly. "If only we knew this Marmaduke's secret," he said.

"We shall," the Toymaker said. "We shall."

"Eh?" said Grumio sharply. "What do you mean? How shall we?"

The Toymaker smiled secretively and sat down at his desk to look through the invoices that always gather at Christmastime, unwanted and uninvited, like distant cousins at a rich man's wake. Grumio shook his head disgustedly and spat on the floor. "You never tell me anything," he muttered, returning to his aborted attempt at threading a needle. The Master Toymaker just laughed.

Each man sat in his own pool of light, divided by sawdust and shadows. The cavernous room was filled with their silence, while all around them dolls' heads, turned this way and that on overhead shelves, seemed to keep watch and whisper one to the other. They saw what the teddy bears, still waiting for their button eyes to be sewn on, could not. Trucks and fire engines and trains ran helter-skelter along tables and shelves, but many were missing wheels and none had a place to go. Enough musical instruments to outfit a band of angels hung from the rafters, yet they made not a sound. The Toymaker's workshop was a place where happiness was in rehearsal and pleasures were remembered or anticipated, but not lived.

Suddenly, there came a knock on the door. The Master Toymaker pulled out his pocket watch, which showed a cat and a fiddle at twelve o'clock, a cow and moon at three. "The cow has not yet jumped over the moon," he said. "They are early."

"They?" asked Grumio.

"This Marmaduke person," said the Toymaker, putting away his watch, "and his puppets—which soon shall be mine. Grumio, run along and sweep up the doll hair in Workshop B while I see to our guests." Blowing on his glasses, the better to study the workings of those remarkable puppets, he made his way slowly toward the door.

"Patience, Mister Marmaduke," the Toymaker called out, for the door was being pounded upon with great vigor. But when it was opened, the Toymaker was surprised to discover not the puppetmaster but three strangers, one in black, and two in rather worn-looking sailor costumes.

"May I help you?"

"We seem to have lost our way, kind sir," said the old man in black, breathing heavily. "Might we rest our weary bones a spell?"

"Well," the Toymaker grumbled, "I'm expecting some guests, but I don't suppose I can turn away three such distinguished-looking gentlemen as yourselves." He waved them in, shut the door, and said, "I am the Master Toymaker. Perhaps you have some children on your Christmas list for whom you have yet to purchase gifts. Do you see something you like, a doll that strikes your fancy, a train that carries you back to your youth? By the way, I didn't catch your names."

"We didn't toss 'em out," said Gonzorgo.

"I am Mister Barnaby. And these are two employees of mine—"

"Yet to be paid," Roderigo muttered.

"—called Roderigo and Gonzorgo. And I am not interested in children's playthings. Truth be told, Master Toymaker, though it might harden your heart against me to hear it, I loathe children. Allow me to confide in you— as I see that you are a person who can be trusted—that I am soon to be wed. Yes, yes, I thank you for your felicitations. But, you see, there is a problem. The darling girl whose good fortune it is to become Missus Barnaby has thirteen brothers and sisters of various sizes and shapes, and there's not a one among them I can abide. And there's not a one among them she'll be parted from. Oh, what I wouldn't give to be rid of the lot of them!"

The Toymaker studied Barnaby carefully before saying what was in his mind. "What exactly *would* you give?" he said at last.

Barnaby was not sure what to make of the Toymaker's question, but was saved from answering it by another knock on the door. "That will be my guests," said the Toymaker. He picked up a bell and rang it. After a moment, Grumio appeared.

"What now?" he snapped irritably.

"Will you take these gentlemen to the next room and give them something to drink, Grumio? Then return to me at once. And Mister Barnaby, do give some thought to my question, won't you?"

Nodding his head uncertainly, Barnaby followed Grumio out of the room. Gonzorgo pulled Roderigo away from a shelf filled with teddy bears, and followed after.

"The poor little creatures," Roderigo said, sniffling. "They don't even have eyes to weep at their misfortune."

At the door stood Delancey Marmaduke, stooping slightly so that his eyes just cleared the sill. "I have the puppets on my cart, Master Toymaker," he said. "Where shall you want them?"

"Bring the cart right in here. This door is extra wide to allow for the delivery of lumber and machinery. Do you need a hand? Good, good, then I'll wait."

A moment later, into the room, pushed by the huffing and puffing puppetmaster, came Alan and Jane, Tom-Tom and Mary, cheeks freshly powdered, lips newly painted. They sat stiffly upon Marmaduke's cart and tried very hard not to blink.

"Marvelous!" the Toymaker exclaimed. "Remarkable! Uncanny! Your own handiwork, you say?"

Marmaduke nodded. "Where is the performance to take place?"

"Well, I . . ." The Toymaker glanced over his shoulder. He did not speak again until his apprentice entered the room. "Here we are, Grumio," he said. "This is the gentleman I was telling you about. And *these* are his puppets. What do you think, hmm?"

Marmaduke cleared his throat. "About the performance," he said.

"Oh, I wish no performance," said the Toymaker.

"But you've already paid."

"And now I pay you even more." He quickly handed Marmaduke a purse full of money.

"But I don't understand," Marmaduke said. "If you don't want the puppets to perform . . ."

"I merely wish you to take this money and go."

"Money? For what?"

"Your puppets. I buy them of you."

"But I don't want to sell them."

"Here is a witness to the sale," the Toymaker said, putting his arm about Grumio's bony shoulders. "You *have* sold them."

"I c-can't," the puppetmaster sputtered. "I haven't the right."

"Be wise," said Grumio. "Take your money and go."

"You don't know what you're buying," said Marmaduke.

The Toymaker slapped his hands together so loudly that Marmaduke jumped. So, in fact, did the "puppets," but fortunately no one noticed. "Enough!" the Toymaker shouted. "You broke our laws by displaying your puppets after you'd been warned. I've treated you fairly. Argue with me any further, and I'll see that you get the full penalty the law will allow. Out of the country with you, and quickly!"

Marmaduke looked uncertainly at Alan. When Alan winked at him, he said, "Well, if you don't like the bargain later on, remember you made it yourself." Then, knowing that his "puppets" were quite capable of taking care of themselves, he bowed to the Toymaker and said, "I bid you good afternoon."

As soon as he'd left, Grumio asked, "Are you going to break them up and see how they're made?"

"I shall dissect them at my leisure," said the Toymaker. "But first I have a more pressing matter to attend to. Come, let us join Mister Barnaby and see if he has thought of an answer to my question."

"Uncle Barnaby, here!" said Jane, as soon as the door to the workshop had closed. "We're in danger of being found out!"

"Don't worry," said Tom-Tom. "With any luck, we'll be broken into pieces before your uncle Barnaby can get to us."

"We *are* in a pickle," Mary said. "And I've never cared much for pickles. What *are* we to do now?"

Alan thought for a moment and said, "I think we should begin by listening at that keyhole."

EIGHT

THE MASTER TOYMAKER REVEALS
HIS GREATEST INVENTION.

CROWDING AROUND the door to the next room, the four friends were able to make out enough of the Toymaker's conversation with Barnaby to realize that the worries they had now were nothing compared to those which were soon to confront them.

"What I mean by my question," the Toymaker was saying, "was that for the right amount of money, I can assure you that you'll have no need to worry about those annoying children again."

"What is the right amount?" asked Barnaby.

"How much do you have with you?"

"A great deal."

"That sounds like the right amount to me."

"But what am I paying for?" Barnaby asked.

"Toys," said the Toymaker. "Oh, I know what you are thinking, but you're wrong. These are no ordinary toys I'm talking about. These are toys that have been charmed with evil spirits. You hate children, Mister Barnaby.

So you have said. Well, so do I. For years, I've despised them for their endless mirth and their boundless energy, their confounded curiosity and their miserable hopefulness. But I teach them to love me so they will accept from me those playthings that will one day destroy them."

"Toys that kill," Barnaby said. "The very thing for the Widow Piper's cherubs."

"My thoughts precisely."

"How horrid," Mary whispered outside the room.

"What's happening now?" Tom-Tom asked Alan, whose eye was at the keyhole.

Alan described the scene. "Roderigo and Gonzorgo are holding open a large sack, which the Toymaker is filling with toy soldiers. They look innocent enough. Yet they cannot be as innocent as they seem."

"What sets them in motion?" Barnaby was asking.

"This music box," the Toymaker answered, holding up a box that resembled a mountain chalet. "The sound of it releases the evil powers contained within the dolls."

"And when they have done?" asked Barnaby. "Is there no way to restore their placid natures?"

"Well," said the Toymaker, "there *is* an antidote. But if you want that . . ." And here he paused meaningfully.

Barnaby scowled. "I've given you everything I have," he said.

"Everything?"

"Everything." Seeing the Toymaker's doubtfulness, Barnaby reached into his coat pocket. "I do have the money I was going to pay Roderigo and Gonzorgo," he said. "I'm sure they won't mind going a little longer without compensation, will you, boys?"

The two sailors lunged for the pouch, which Barnaby quickly jerked away. "Good," he said. "Here." And he handed it to the Toymaker who, in turn, held up a small vial.

"Inside," said the Toymaker, "is a magic powder. All you have to do is sprinkle it in the air, and, as it settles on the toys, their wickedness will

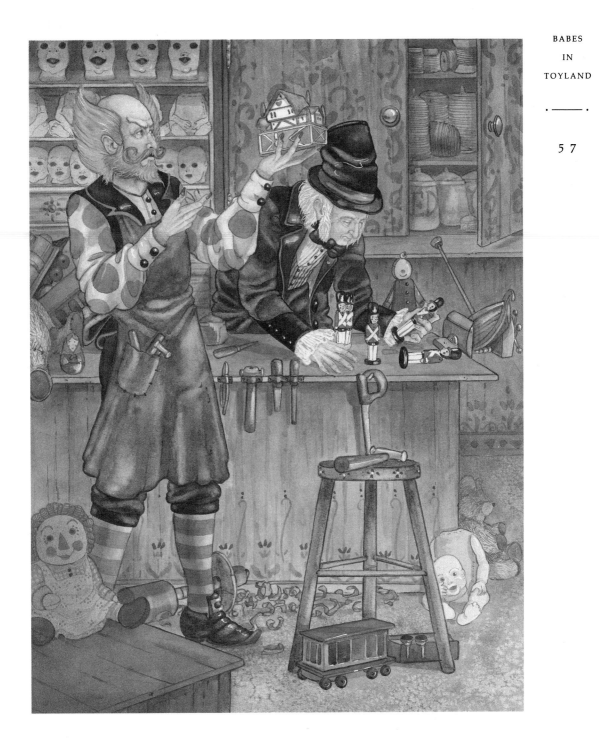

leave them. They will once again be as you see them now—the harmless playthings of children.''

"Only the children will be quite dead,'' said Barnaby. ''Merry Christmas!'' And he chuckled nastily. As he was about to leave, a thought occurred to him. ''How do I know they're going to work?'' he said to the Toymaker. ''It seems to me that for all the money I've paid, a demonstration is in order.''

The Toymaker readily agreed, eager to have an audience for what was,

in his view, his greatest invention. Taking from their boxes the half-dozen toy soldiers that remained in his possession, he placed them on the table and picked up a music box. He took its key in hand and slowly began to wind it.

The six soldiers sat stiffly, side by wooden side, their bayonets and rifles at the ready. And then, as the tinkly music played, their painted eyes came to life. Their arms and legs twitched; their weapons jabbed the air menacingly. All at once, their heads jerked upward, and they were staring into the eyes of the Master Toymaker. As one body, they rose and took aim.

"Stop!" the Toymaker cried as the soldiers mounted their attack. "Something's gone wrong! Help!" But Barnaby worried only about saving himself. "Run!" he called out to Roderigo and Gonzorgo. "And don't drop that sack of toys." Flinging open the door, he fairly bowled over the startled foursome on the other side. Seeing them, he cried, "Alan and Jane! What are you doing here? And Mary, beloved Mary! Come with me, my child! Save yourself!" But Mary did not budge. She was too frightened, both of the dolls that had run amok in the next room and of having been recognized by Mister Barnaby.

"Come on, old man," said Gonzorgo, grabbing Barnaby's arm. "It isn't safe here. Let's go." And the sailors whisked him away.

"We must stop the toy soldiers," Jane said. "They're killing the Toymaker and his apprentice."

"But how?" said Tom-Tom. "Without the antidote—"

"There it is," cried Alan, pointing to something lying on the floor nearby. "It must have dropped from Uncle Barnaby's pocket as he fled. I'll try to save them. You three save yourselves. Hurry now! Wait for me outside."

"Oh, Alan," said Mary. "Do be careful."

Alan looked into Mary's eyes. "Then you do care for me," he said.

But before Mary could answer, Tom-Tom hurried her and Jane off to safety.

The three waited for what felt an eternity but was in fact only a matter of some minutes, worrying about the safety of their friend and brother. When at last Alan appeared in the door of the Toymaker's house, they were relieved to see him alive, yet taken aback by the horror that was written on his face.

"I was able to calm the dolls," he told them, "but too late to help the Toymaker and his apprentice. The dolls have accomplished what they set out to do."

"What is that you're carrying?" Tom-Tom asked.

Alan held up the vial. "What remains of the antidote," he said. "We must see that the dolls Uncle Barnaby intends to give to your brothers and sisters are returned to a state of innocence before they can do any harm. But *first*, you three must leave Toyland."

"We won't leave without you," Mary insisted. "It wouldn't be fair."

"I'll follow soon," said Alan. "We can't let Uncle Barnaby get you, Mary. And I'd feel better if Jane were home, too. We'll wait until darkness falls. Then you three will slip across the border while I, under cover of night, seek out Uncle Barnaby and destroy the evil he wants to unleash."

The four friends said nothing then. They were thinking, perhaps, that Barnaby did not need charmed toys to bring evil into the world. For evil, it seemed, was a part of his nature. And they could not help but wonder if, even with a magic powder, Alan would be quite safe.

NINE

IN WHICH ALAN FINDS HIMSELF A FUGITIVE
FROM JUSTICE, AND MARY BECOMES
A PAWN IN A DEADLY GAME.

BY DUSK, word was out that the Toymaker and his apprentice had been killed, and, as no one without a passport was allowed to leave Toyland until the murderer had been found, the country's borders were being carefully guarded. A hunt was already on for the suspect whose name and description had been supplied by witnesses.

"Alan!" Jane cried, spotting a wanted poster. "You are accused of murder!"

"I?"

"Yes, listen. 'The culprit is' . . . blah, blah, blah . . . it describes you to a tee. And then it says, 'When apprehended, the villain is to be convicted without trial for the heinous crime of murdering Toyland's favorite citizen, the kind and gentle Master Toymaker.'"

"Kind and gentle? Hmph!" Mary said, with disgust. "Let them have eavesdropped within his walls as we have done, and they'd know how kind and gentle was their beloved Toymaker."

"What matters now is that we must protect Alan," said Tom-Tom. "All of Toyland is looking for him."

"It's Mary I worry about," Alan said.

"We are all in some danger, it seems," said Jane. "If only we could leave this place at once."

"There's little chance of that, with the borders being so carefully watched," Mary said.

"We could get through if we had passports," said Alan.

"But how shall we get passports with your name and description on every pillar and post in the land?" Mary asked.

"I'll disguise myself. I've already succeeded as a gypsy and a puppet soldier. Why not something else like . . . like . . . that fellow over there?" Alan pointed at a raggedy scarecrow.

"There's nothing to lose in trying," Tom-Tom agreed. "Let's hide ourselves in that barn and get a night's sleep. In the morning, we three, accompanied by our friend the scarecrow, will appear at the Courthouse door, passport applications in hand."

By the time the first rooster announced the day's dawning, Alan had already exchanged clothing with the scarecrow. The others told him that he needn't worry about being discovered, for he now resembled one of those unfortunates whom the rest of humanity passes by each day without so much as a glance. The scarecrow, on the other hand, had been transformed into quite a dashing military figure, commanding his post with new authority and style.

Stealing cautiously into town, the foursome arrived at the Courthouse just as it was opening.

"You don't look a bit like the police description," Jane assured her brother.

"That is because I'm now a handyman," said Alan.

"And I," said Jane, modeling her slightly altered puppet costume, "am a lady's maid."

"I'm a butler," Tom-Tom said.

Mary drew herself to her full height and proclaimed in a sonorous voice,

"I am Lady Edwina Flaffingdale, a rich eccentric who wears gentlemen's military clothing and employs riffraff such as your lowly selves." Then, laughing nervously, she added, "Oh, I do hope we succeed."

"We will," said Alan, "if we stick together."

With great determination, into the Courthouse they marched.

Once inside, Mary, in her nervousness, grew faint. Frightened that she would pass out at any moment and give the game away, she excused herself and went outside the Courthouse door.

And then a most unfortunate occurrence took place. For just as she had regained her equilibrium and was turning to go back inside, a hand reached out and grabbed her.

"Oh!" Mary cried, face-to-face with her captor. "It's you!"

"Behold," said Barnaby, "your long-lost fiancé. It's a fine morning for a wedding."

"Whose wedding?" Mary asked. She was starting to feel faint again.

"Ours."

"It may be a fine morning for a wedding," she said, rallying herself. "But it's a 'good morning' for you."

"Somebody waiting in there for you?" Barnaby asked.

"Yes," Mary said. "That is, no. I'm alone."

Barnaby pulled Mary to him. "I'll be short and sweet with you, Mistress Mary. There's a marriage bureau next to the courtroom. We'll be married there at once or . . ."

"Or what?"

"I'll hand Alan over. No, don't protest. I know he's in there. His disguise may fool some people, but it cannot fool me. In a moment, the Royal Court will condemn him for killing the Toymaker and his apprentice. Don't forget, there were witnesses."

"And who might they be?" Mary asked.

Barnaby smiled sweetly. "Your humble servant," he said. "It's my duty. He has disgraced the family. He's an assassin. But for your sake, my darling wife-to-be, I'll let him escape."

"What about the other witnesses?"

"Roderigo and Gonzorgo, you mean?" Barnaby laughed. "They can be bought for the price of a meal, and not even one of three courses. See, here they come now."

Mary turned and saw two gentlemen approaching. She recognized their sailor suits but would not have known who they were otherwise because of the hoods they wore over their heads.

"We have taken employment as royal executioners of Toyland," Roderigo informed Barnaby and Mary, "as our earlier employment offered travel as its sole compensation."

"What is that you're carrying?" Barnaby asked.

"It is the warrant for Master Alan," Gonzorgo growled.

"Let me see it," Mary said.

"Better not," said Roderigo. "It's pretty gloomy reading."

"I am sure it will be cheerier than a marriage license," Mary said, and she took the warrant from Gonzorgo's hands.

"There'll be about two hours of painful preliminaries," said Gonzorgo as Mary muttered, "Hot irons . . . the rack . . . flogging . . . oh, dear." She was quite pale as she handed the paper back to Gonzorgo and turned to Barnaby.

"Do you promise you won't turn Alan in?" she said.

"If."

"Yes, yes—*if* I agree to marry you."

"At once."

"At once."

"Then you have my solemn oath, my beloved," Barnaby said.

Mary turned to the door of the Courthouse and bid her dear Alan a silent, tearful good-bye. Then, turning back, she said, "You may have my hand, Mister Barnaby, but never my heart."

"I'll take what I can get," said Barnaby.

Moments later, Alan and Jane and Tom-Tom emerged from the Courthouse. And Mary was gone.

TEN

WITH THE ANNOUNCEMENT OF TWO MARRIAGES COME BETRAYAL AND DESPAIR.

"'WE HAVE THE PASSPORTS,'' Alan said, outside the Courthouse. "Now all we need is Mary."

"Where can she be?" asked Jane.

"There's quite a crowd gathering in the square," Tom-Tom commented. "And it's not a friendly one. Look at those placards."

"Bring the Culprit to Justice!" read one angry sign. "Hang the Evil Alan!" read another. "Avenge the Murder of the Master Toymaker!" a third proclaimed.

"Oh, Alan," Jane said, "these people mean business. If they discover you . . ." She let her thought trail off, not wanting to follow it to its frightening conclusion.

"We can't leave without Mary," said Alan.

"But, look!" Jane cried. "Here she comes. With Uncle Barnaby!"

Barnaby was beaming as he strolled through the village square with Contrary Mary on his arm. Even downcast, she was radiantly beautiful. It was little wonder that he looked a trifle smug to have claimed such a prize as his bride.

Mary's eyes caught Alan's. Sorrow welled up in her as she forced herself to look down, fearful that she would give Alan away. But Barnaby noticed their exchange of glances, and he smiled to himself just before he called out, "Officer! Oh, officer!"

A policeman came running. "See here, constable," said Barnaby. "This man you're looking for, the one called Alan." Mary's eyes widened in alarm.

"Yes?" said the policeman.

"Well, there he is." And he pointed a gnarled finger at the ragtag figure next to the Courthouse door.

Mary attempted to bolt from Barnaby's side as the officer went at once to arrest Alan, but Barnaby pulled her in. "You promised," she hissed.

"I know, my dear," said Barnaby. "And it grieves me to do what I have done. But one's duties as a citizen must come before one's conjugal vows, whatever the circumstances. Besides, I understand that a reward has been offered. And, as you didn't bring a dowry to help get our marriage off to a proper start, we must seek what funds we can where we find them."

Mary dropped her head and said not another word. Her fate was sealed. So, it seemed, was Alan's.

In no time at all, Alan found himself standing before the Royal Judge.

"Hear ye! Hear ye!" the Judge cried out. "The Royal Court does herewith, without due process of law and in the presence of these good and loyal subjects of the Unincorporated State of Toyland, find the outlaw Alan guilty of the murders of the Master Toymaker and his apprentice, Grumio, and orders that he be executed in the manner prescribed by Law and Most Royal Whim, forthwith, posthaste, and at once!"

A cheer rang out from the crowd, nearly drowning out Jane's cries on behalf of her brother and Mary's sobs for her beloved. Tom-Tom raised an angry fist and decried the Judge's decree, but his protest was to no avail. The Royal Judge pounded his gavel and brought the crowd to silence.

"Unless," he continued, "*unless* he, meaning the outlaw Alan, chooses

to take advantage of the law that gives every condemned man the right to plead the benefit of widow."

"The benefit of widow?" Alan asked softly. "What is that?"

"Silence!" the Judge bellowed. "I'll fine you for contempt of court if you insist on asking questions before I can answer them." Then, clearing his throat, he went on to explain, "Any widow may claim a condemned man for her second husband, and he shall be *free* as long as he supports said widow and saves her from becoming a charge upon the state."

"Never!" Alan cried. "I'll die rather than marry anybody but Contrary Mary."

Barnaby stepped forward and said, "If you mean Missus Barnaby, you're a little late, I'm afraid."

Alan regarded Mary with disbelief. "You've married Uncle Barnaby?" he said.

Feeling both rage and despair, Mary replied, "He recognized me, but swore to let you escape if I married him at once. Oh, Alan, forgive me. I did it only for you."

"Then bring on the widows!" Alan cried. "I will marry for Mary's sake. And live to square accounts with you, Uncle!"

"You don't frighten me, lad," said Barnaby, pulling an old toothpick from his pocket and applying it to his teeth.

The Judge pounded his gavel once more, and called out, "Let the widows of the land be summoned!"

Alan waited anxiously with Tom-Tom and Jane for the better part of an hour. From time to time, the Judge glanced up from his game of solitaire to the clock on the courtroom wall. Each time, he turned in Alan's direction, shook his head, and returned to his cards.

"Don't despair," Tom-Tom said at last. "Somebody will find you worth taking."

"You make him sound like a chipped plate at a tag sale," said Jane. And she began to cry.

"Don't worry, dear sister," Alan said. "We've been through worse than this. We lost our parents at a tender age, we were almost drowned at sea, we've learned that our uncle has tried to have us murdered. And, each time, we've come through."

"You're right," Jane said. "We mustn't lose hope yet. Through these courtroom doors will step a widow: your wife-to-be and your salvation."

Almost on cue, the doors opened. A large woman, with braids of red hair and a strange cap, stepped into the room, nearly making the walls quake with each step she took. "I am here," she sang out in a full, round voice.

A court clerk scrambled in through the door behind her and informed the packed courtroom, "Madame Gertrude is the only widow left in Toyland. She has come here today with the greatest reluctance, for, after an unhappy first marriage, she is in no rush to wed again."

"My first husband was tone-deaf," Madame Gertrude explained. "For an opera singer to have a tone-deaf husband is the greatest curse."

"You understand," said the Royal Judge, "that Alan is a murderer."

"As long as he isn't tone-deaf," Madame Gertrude said. "Where is he?"

"I'm doomed," Alan muttered under his breath. "I can't carry a tune in a bucket."

"Courage," Tom-Tom said. And, rising, he announced, "Madame Gertrude, allow me to introduce you to your future husband, Signor Alan, most recently engaged by the Venusian Opera."

"A singer!" Madame Gertrude cried, rushing over to take Alan's hand in hers. "The moment I laid eyes on you, I knew you were a singer. A tenor, yes?"

"Just in the shower," Alan replied. "When the water's too cold."

"Come, let me hear you. Your voice shall be the test."

"And I have already failed," Alan said to himself. He eyed Roderigo and Gonzorgo in their black hoods and thought of the fate awaiting him.

The courtroom crowd fell into silence. Alan cleared his throat several times and was about to begin singing when Madame Gertrude asked, "Do you know that aria in E minor by Korfalottski?"

"Why, no," Alan replied. "I thought I would sing the aria in A major by Lottanervski."

"I've never heard it," said Madame Gertrude.

"And you never will again," Alan muttered as he broke into song.

Had his "aria" been set down on the page, it would have been seen that Alan completed no more than four bars before Madame Gertrude ran screaming from the room. "Never!" she cried. "Let him hang!" And she was gone.

Alan shook his head sadly. "There's no hope for me now," he said as Jane and Tom-Tom came to comfort him. He looked out into the crowd and saw Mary wipe a tear from her eye.

Just then, the door to the courtroom flew open again, and through it came the Widow Piper and twelve of her children. Tom-Tom's eyes lit up.

"Mother!" he cried, rushing to her. "*You* are a widow! You must marry Alan."

"Don't be ridiculous," the Widow Piper said. "Why would I do such a thing? And, Tom-Tom, where have you been? I've looked all over Toyland for Mary and you."

"There's no time for that now, Mother. You must marry Alan to save him. Children, help me! Make Mother see."

Bo Peep looked up at her big brother and said, "I don't know why you want Mother to marry Alan, Tom-Tom, but it's too late."

"Too late?"

"Yes," said Sulky Sue. "We told her not to bother."

"But she didn't listen," Peter said, "and got us a new father."

The Widow Piper grinned widely. "It's true, Tom-Tom," she said. "I've just been married in the room next door. Here is my husband now."

And in walked Delancey Marmaduke.

ELEVEN

WHEREIN MISTER BARNABY DOES A GOOD DEED.

TOM-TOM WASN'T SURE which shocked him more—the news that he had a stepfather or the certainty of Alan's impending doom.

Delancey Marmaduke smiled at Tom-Tom. "I hope you'll have me for a father, my boy," he said. "When your mother and I collided, it was love at first sight."

"After we'd picked ourselves up off the street," the Widow Piper said, with a laugh.

"But what's going on here?" Marmaduke asked. "Have they caught the Master Toymaker's murderer?"

"Yes," Jane said, stifling a sob. "And now he's to be executed."

When Delancey Marmaduke was made to realize that the falsely accused murderer was none other than one of his favorite "puppets," he was outraged. He spoke out in Alan's behalf, but the Judge would not listen to reason.

"There were witnesses," he told Marmaduke. "And if you know what's good for you, you'll say no more." Then, rising, he proclaimed in a loud voice, "Let the execution commence!"

Roderigo and Gonzorgo, for their parts, were nervously studying the warrant. "I can't do it," Roderigo moaned. "Torture, the rack, flogging. It isn't in my nature, Gonzorgo. It'll put me off my food for days."

"I could do it," Gonzorgo said, "if I'd had some practice. We may have convinced the Royal Judge we are professional executioners, but now that it's come down to it, I'm afraid we'll make fools of ourselves. Come on, let's have a word with Alan."

As Alan saw the two hooded figures approach, his face grew pale. When they grasped him on either shoulder, his knees began to give way. And when they began to whisper in either ear, he was sure these were the last words he would ever hear.

"We're in a very embarrassing position," Gonzorgo confided. "And only you can help us out. When we start to execute you, everybody is liable to laugh."

"I won't," Alan promised.

"But there's such a lot of it," Roderigo said. He began to enumerate the various stages of torture required by the state.

"Oh, dear!" Alan cried. "I won't be able to live through all that!"

"Then, since you've got to leave this cold, hard world anyway, won't you allow us to send you our way?" Roderigo asked. "We'll make it much pleasanter, we promise."

Alan nodded. "Whatever you say," he said.

"Wise lad," said Gonzorgo. "Now, what would you like in the way of a last meal?"

Alan gazed across the room at Mary. "All I can think of," he said, "is angel food cake."

"And a glass of wine?" asked Gonzorgo.

"Yes," Alan said. "That'll be all."

"Good," Gonzorgo said to Roderigo as they left the room. "We'll put some poison in his wine, and he'll be dead before the irons are even hot."

"Or the rack is ready," said Roderigo. "What a relief!"

While they waited, Jane and Tom-Tom, the Widow Piper, her twelve children and new husband, Delancey Marmaduke, gathered round Alan to tell him good-bye. Jane's tears flowed as she kissed her brother's cheeks. Tom-Tom assured Alan that he and Jane would soon be wed and that he would always take good care of her. Only Mary did not come forward, for Barnaby held her wrist so tightly she could not move. Alan's eyes searched her out, but her head was lowered. She did not want him to see her crying and carry that image of her to his grave.

Soon, Roderigo and Gonzorgo reentered with Alan's cake and wine. As they passed through the crowd, Mary kicked Barnaby's shin and ran toward her beloved. Barnaby quickly followed, catching her just as she was about to reach Alan.

"There, there, my sweet little wife," he said. "I know this isn't easy for you. But think how hard it is for *me*!"

"For you?" Mary cried.

"Certainly. I have done my duty, as any good citizen would have done, but to condemn one's own flesh and blood to death is a grievous task. My heart is heavy, dearest Mary."

"As it should be," Mary said bitterly.

"Do not be so harsh to your loving husband," said Barnaby. "Such treatment is difficult to bear . . . without help." And here he reached for the glass of wine that was passing by. Before Roderigo could stop him, Barnaby had downed its contents in one quick gulp.

"Fool!" Gonzorgo cried. "Now we'll never be paid."

With one hand, Barnaby grasped his throat; with the other, he released Mary's arm. He tried to speak, but the only sound he seemed able to produce was an unpleasant rasp. Dropping to the ground, he waved his arms about frantically. Then all motion ceased. And he was silent.

"He's overcome with grief," said the Widow Piper.

Mary knelt down by him. "It isn't that," she said, her voice trembling. "The old man has finally done a good deed. Oh, Alan! I'm a widow!" Never were these words proclaimed so rapturously. "Will you marry me, dearest?"

"I thought you'd never ask," Alan replied.

Mary rushed to him and kissed him tearfully. But now her tears were tears of joy. "We'll go to the marriage bureau at once," Alan said.

"We'll go with you," Tom-Tom said, taking Jane's hand. "That is," he said, "if you'll have me."

"Oh, Tom-Tom," said Jane.

The Judge looked down at the proceedings, banged his gavel once, and said, "Case dismissed."

Just as they were about to leave the courtroom, Mary noticed her brothers and sisters gathered round a large bag that was leaning against a wall.

"Look," Bo Peep cried. She held a fancily wrapped box up to view. "It says, 'Merry Christmas, Bo Peep.' Oh, Mother, may I open it? It's only a few days till Christmas."

"But who is it from?" the Widow Piper asked.

"I don't know," Bo Peep replied. "But Simple Simon has already opened his."

"It's a music box," Simon said, winding its key.

"Stop!" Alan shouted. "Simon, don't let go of the key!"

"But why, Alan?" the boy said. "I want to hear the music."

"These are the toys Uncle Barnaby bought from the Master Toymaker. You mustn't play with them."

By now, most of the boxes were opened, and in each child's hand was a wooden soldier. Just as Simon was about to let go of the key, Alan found in his pocket what he was desperately searching for—the vial containing the

magic dust! He opened it quickly and scattered its contents over the heads of the children. As the dust fell on all the toys, the music started to play.

Alan held his breath. The soldiers' eyes flickered with life. Their arms and legs began to twitch. And then they grew still.

"What's the matter, Alan?" asked Bo Peep. "You look so scared."

"They're only toys," Tommy Tucker said. And all the children laughed.

Now, when Alan removed the curse from the Toymaker's toys, an amazing thing happened. The last remaining vestiges of evil in all of Toyland disappeared. And the toys, of which there were a very many in this place, all came to life, as if to celebrate the good that is in toys—and boys and girls—everywhere.

After Alan married Mary and Tom-Tom married Jane, they came out from the Courthouse into the village square to discover that Toyland was filled with magic. Balloons flew through the air of their own accord.

Dolls in pretty starched dresses sat on wooden chairs, laughing and having tea out of pink and blue cups. Stuffed elephants paraded down the streets with teddy bears on their backs. And toy soldiers marched to the sound of tiny tin bugles and little snare drums.

Everywhere, Toyland was alive with the spirit of Christmas, a spirit that had been long forgotten while evil was in the land.

EPILOGUE

NEW LIVES ARE BEGUN,
PAST JOYS REMEMBERED.

SHORTLY AFTER CHRISTMAS, Mary and Alan and Tom-Tom and Jane returned to their homeland, but the Widow Piper and her twelve remaining children stayed in Toyland to help Delancey Marmaduke in his new position as Master Toymaker. To this day, whenever they apply the final coat of paint to a bright red fire engine or tie the last ribbon on a cherry-cheeked doll, they smile to think of the happiness of the children who will open these toys on Christmas mornings in far-off lands.

And they smile to remember the time when the toy soldiers marched.

*The illustrations in this book were done on 100% rag Crescent illustration board
in watercolor with a light glaze effect, building up colors in thin washes.
The text type was set via the Linotron 202 in Palatino by Maryland Linotype
Composition Company, Baltimore, Maryland.
The title display type was hand-lettered by Linda Harper.
Color separations were made by Heinz Weber, Inc., Los Angeles, California.
Printed by Holyoke Lithograph, Springfield, Massachusetts
Bound by A. Horowitz & Sons Bookbinders, Fairfield, New Jersey
Production supervision by Warren Wallerstein and Eileen McGlone
Typography, binding, and endpaper design by Joy Chu*